All-Action Animal Art

WHALES, SHARKS, AND DOLPHINS

I0805119

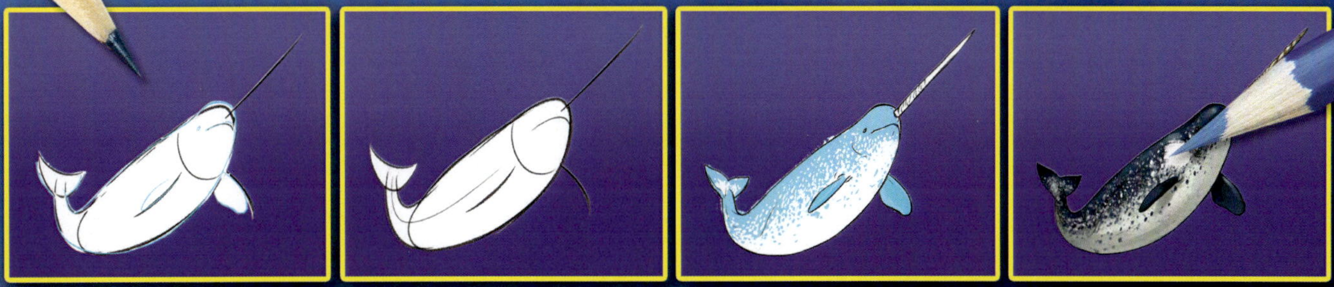

PowerKiDS press

Juan Calle & William Potter

Published in 2019 by **The Rosen Publishing Group, Inc.**
29 East 21st Street, New York, NY 10010

Cataloging-in-Publication Data

Names: Calle, Juan. | Potter, William.
Title: Whales, sharks, and dolphins / Juan Calle and William Potter.
Description: New York : PowerKids Press, 2019. | Series: All-action animal art | Includes glossary and index.
Identifiers: ISBN 9781538347485 (pbk.) | ISBN 9781538347508 (library bound) | ISBN 9781538347492 (6pack)
Subjects: LCSH: Marine animals in art--Juvenile literature. | Drawing--Technique--Juvenile literature.
Classification: LCC NC781.C355 2019 | DDC 743.6--dc23

Copyright © Arcturus Holdings Ltd, 2019

Art by Juan Calle, Color by Luis Suarez (Liberum Donum)
Text by William Potter
Edited by Joe Harris and Sebastian Rydberg, with Julia Adams
Designed by Emma Randall

All rights reserved. No part of this book may be reproduced in any form without permission in writing from the publisher, except by a reviewer.

Manufactured in the United States of America

CPSIA Compliance Information: Batch CWPK19: For Further Information contact Rosen Publishing, New York, New York at 1-800-237-9932.

CONTENTS

GETTING STARTED

THE STEPS

This book shows how you can draw a realistic sea creature starting with simple shapes. You can then add in detail, such as fins, tails, and scales.

WHAT YOU NEED

To follow the steps in this book, all you need is some paper, a pencil (with sharpener), an eraser, paintbrushes, and water-based paint.

The first two steps show the basic building blocks for the body—circles, ovals, and curved lines—and the position of fins.

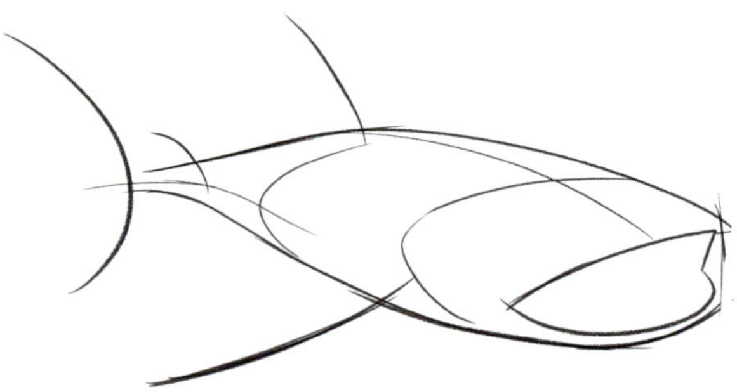

The third step refines these simple shapes and adds detail, such as the eyes and mouth. New lines are in blue as a guide. When you have drawn these outlines, you can erase the working lines you drew in steps 1 and 2.

Later steps add extra detail, including gills, teeth, and skin patterns.

The final step is a guide to what shades you should use to complete your picture.

RELATIVE SIZES

If you want to draw several whales and sharks together in one picture, here's a handy chart that compares their sizes.

The adult sperm whale is roughly twice as long as the adult orca.

The whale shark is the world's largest fish.

The largest animal that ever lived is the blue whale. Its heart is the size of a small car.

The narwhal's tusk can grow to be half its body length.

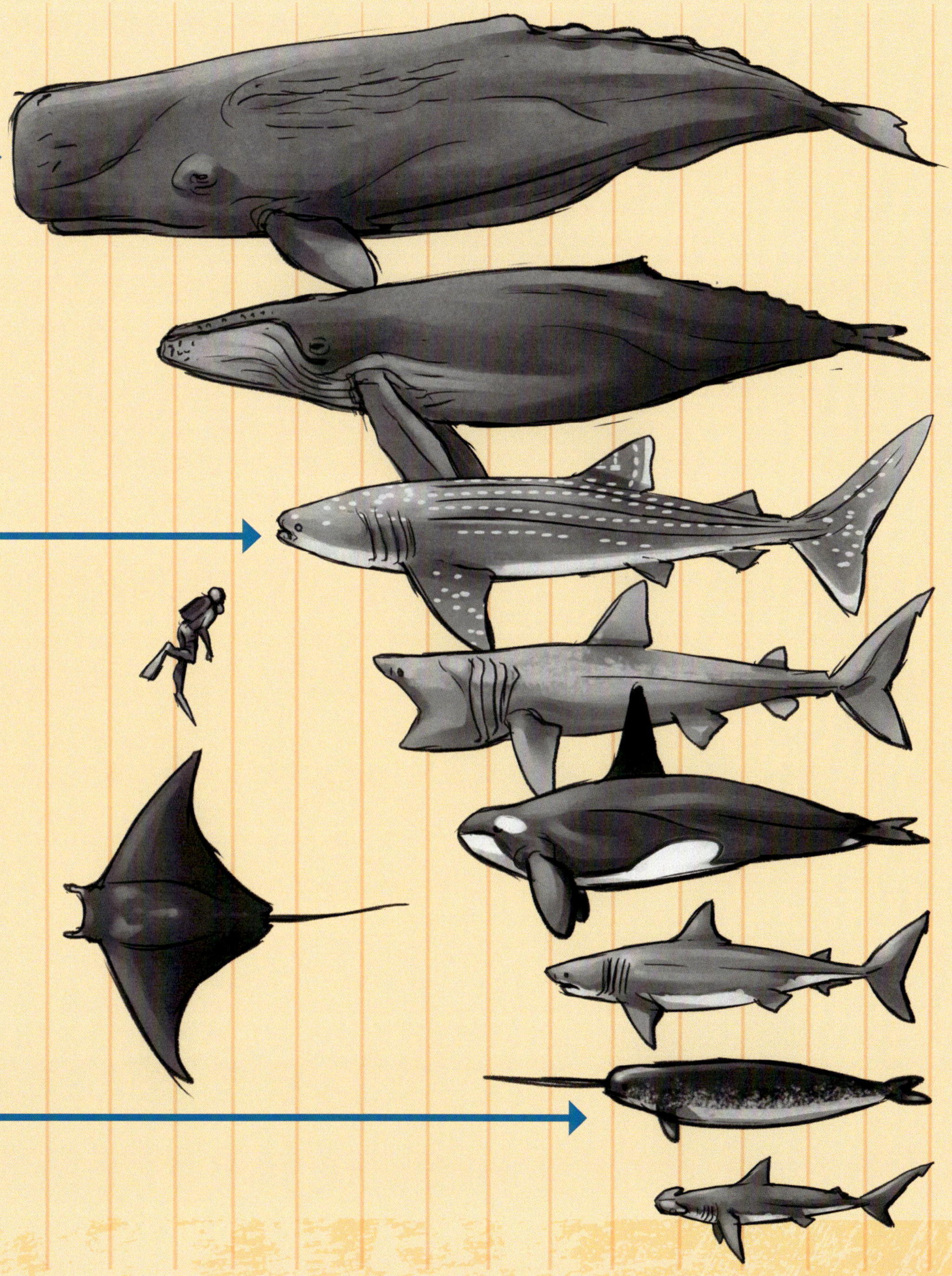

SPERM WHALE

This giant of the deep sea has a rectangular head.

1. Draw a slightly curved sausage shape, with a wide flat end for the head and a point toward the back.

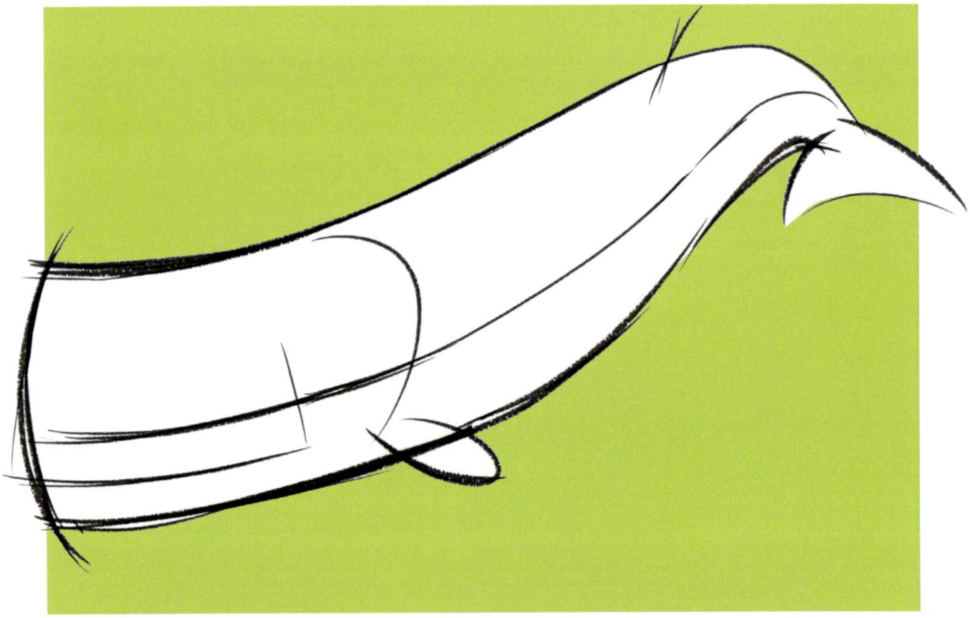

2. Add a tail fin and a small pectoral fin. Use lines to mark the mouth and the location of the eye.

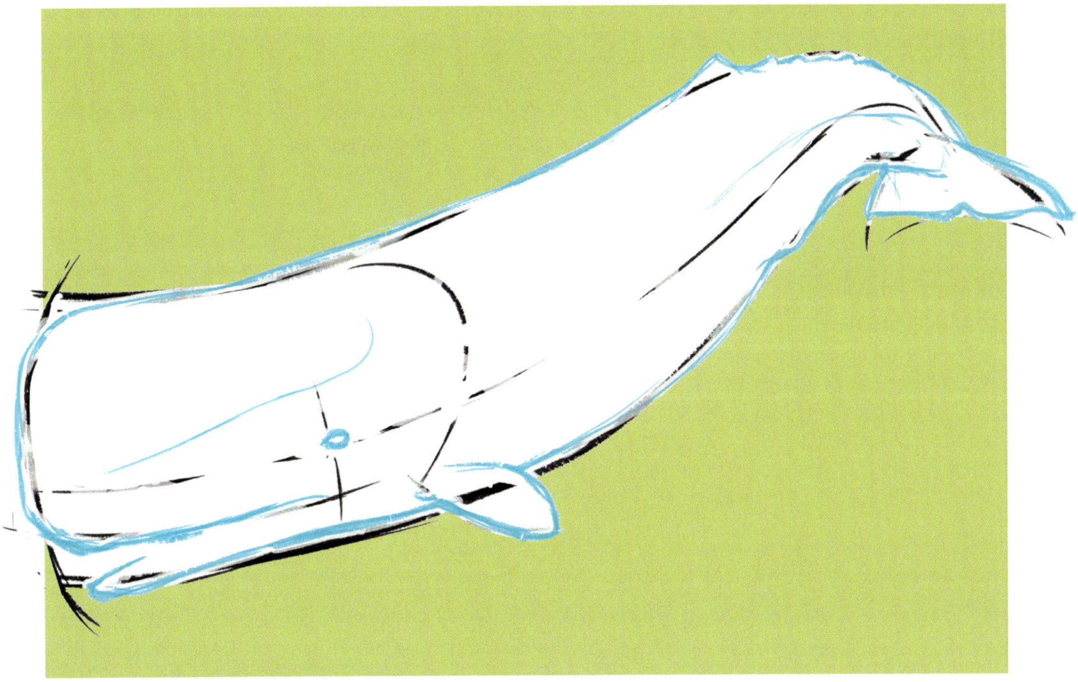

3. Add small bumps on the back, a triangle notch in the tail fin, and a tiny eye just behind and above the mouth.

4. Use short lines to mark wrinkles on the whale's skin, then add teeth in the open mouth.

TOP TIP

The sperm whale has wrinkly skin. Use light tones, called highlights, where the sun lights the upper edges. Add shadows below to bring out the shape of these skin folds.

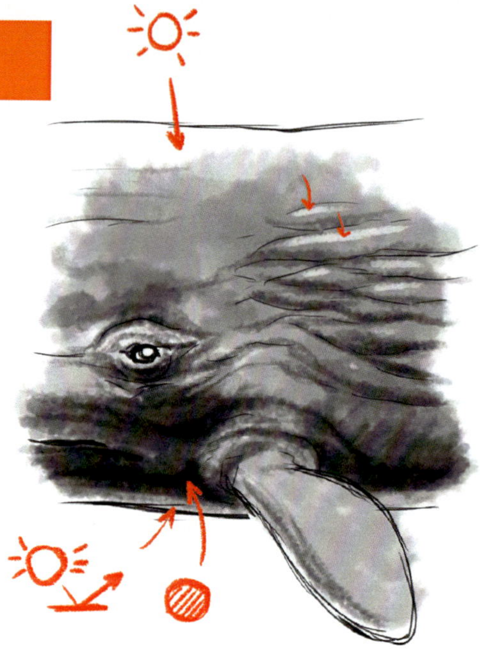

5. Paint your sperm whale in dark blue tones, then add a paler blue shine along its upper body and the top edge of the fins.

DOLPHIN

This acrobatic marine mammal is launching itself out of the water.

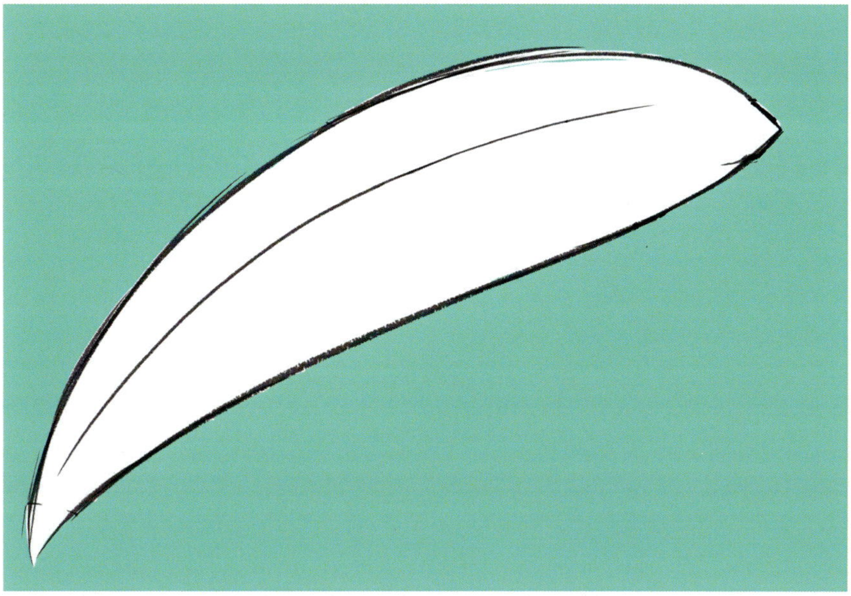

1. Sketch a slightly curved fish shape.

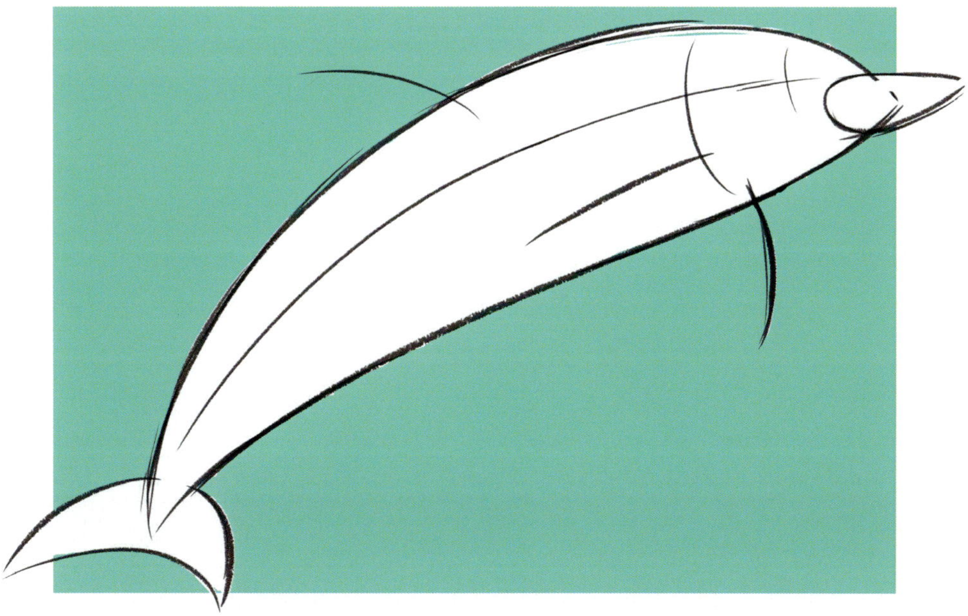

2. Add a pointed nose and crescent tail fin. Mark the head, the nose, and where the other fins will go.

3. Shape the dorsal and pectoral fins. Position the eye, and draw a line for the dolphin's mouth.

4. Erase your working lines, then mark the edges of this common dolphin's dark patterns.

TOP TIP

To draw splashing water, follow the movement of the dolphin, making the water's edges curve away from its body. Give the splash a rippled edge, adding a few extra drips.

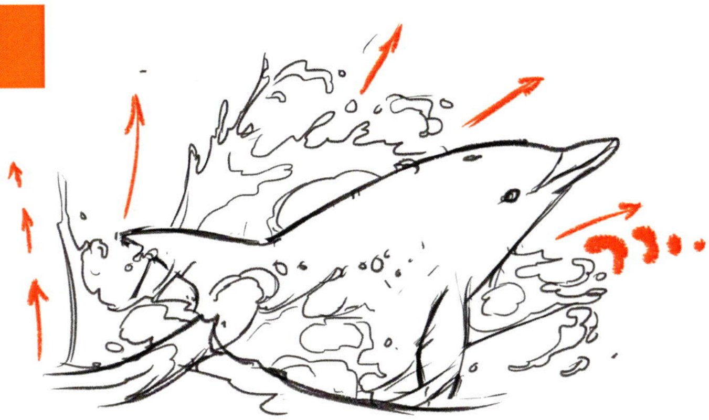

5. Paint the dark areas, then paint the pale areas with a tan shade. You could add a splash of water below the leaping dolphin.

HAMMERHEAD SHARK

This striking sea predator has an odd-looking flat head with eyes on either end.

1. Outline an oval with pointed ends for the body.

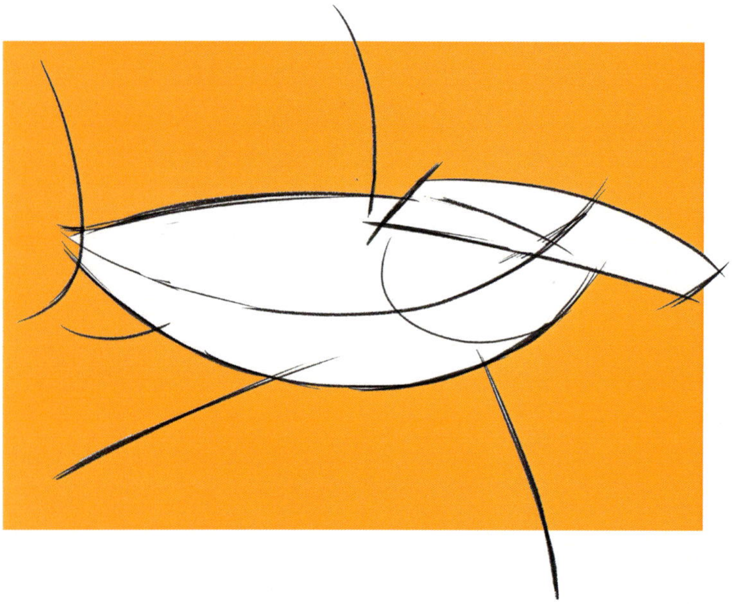

2. Indicate the fin positions. Add a curved rectangle for the head.

3. Shape the triangular fins. Add a rippled edge to the front of the head and an eye at one end. Draw an open mouth below the head.

4. Add the back fins and then the five gill slits behind the head. Draw the sharp teeth, then add lines dividing the front of the head.

WILD FACT!

The bizarre shape of this shark's head is thought to help it locate weak electrical signals given off by its prey.

5. Paint this shark using a bright blue with a paler blue on its underside. Add highlights to the head and fins.

MANTA RAY

This gentle giant has a large mouth for scooping up tiny plankton.

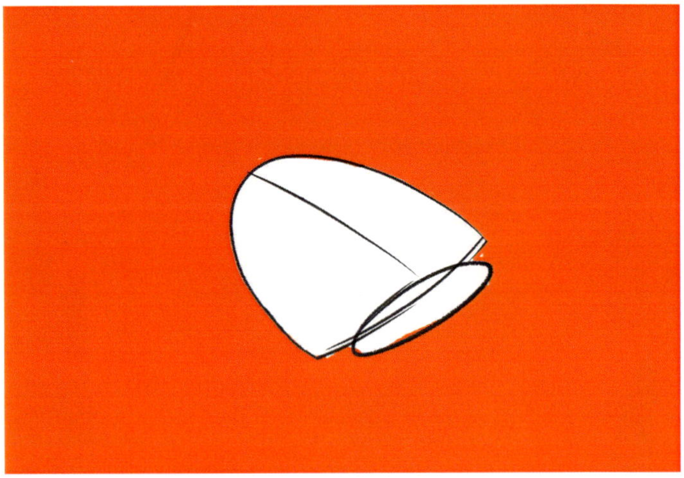

1. To form the manta ray's body, draw a half-oval shape. Add the outline of the open mouth at the flat end.

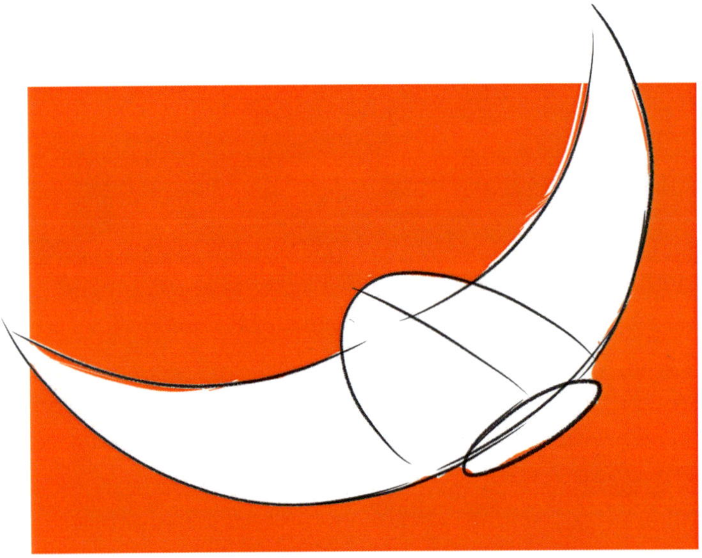

2. Sketch a crescent for the manta's huge pectoral fins.

3. Draw a tiny eye at the side of the head. Now draw the small fins below the mouth, which help it scoop up food, and a tiny dorsal fin on its back.

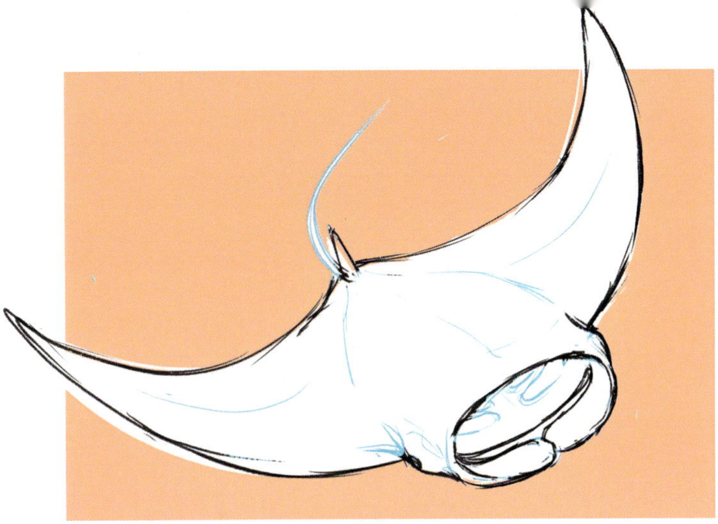

4. Draw the manta ray's thin tail, dividing lines on both pectoral fins, and the detail inside the mouth.

5. Mark the dark and light patches on the manta ray's body. The ray is dark on top and white on its belly.

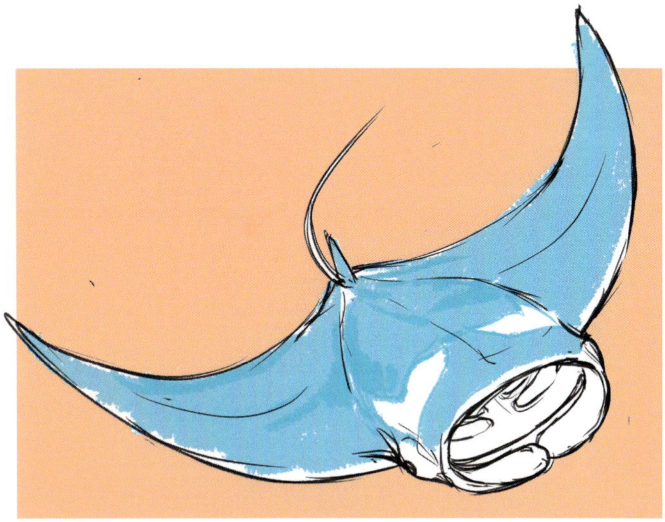

6. Use inky blue-black paint for the dark areas on the ray, leaving the fin tips, eyes, mouth, and symmetrical patches on either side of the head a pale blue.

ORCA

The orca, or killer whale, is a large whale with a striking black-and-white pattern.

1. Draw a small oval for the head and a large oval for the body, tapering to form a tail.

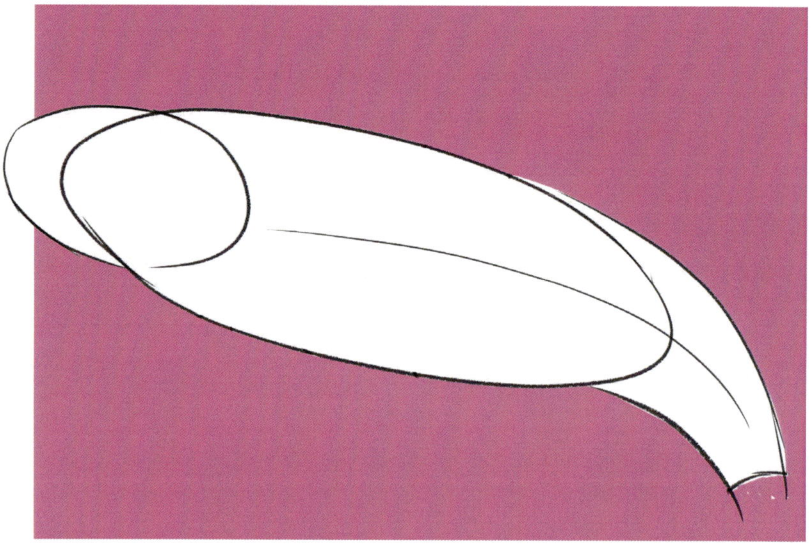

2. Add a tall dorsal fin above, two paddle-shaped flippers below, and a wide tail fin.

3. Mark the open mouth, and add a tiny eye just above where the jaws meet. Add a curve in the tail.

4. Erase your working lines and add some definition to the body, plus short, sharp teeth in the upper jaw.

5. Mark up the black areas on the orca's body, leaving a white belly and white spot behind the eye.

WILD FACT!

Like wolf packs, orcas work in teams to catch prey. They are often called "wolves of the sea."

HUMPBACK WHALE

This huge, bumpy humpback is swimming to the surface for air.

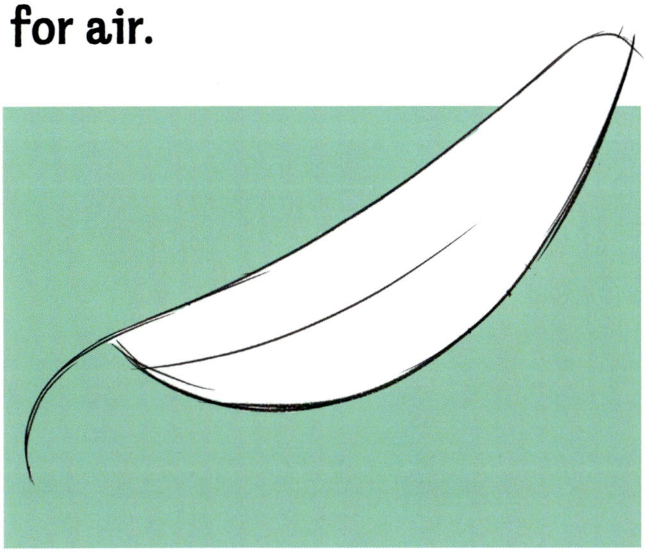

1. Draw a wide smile shape for the whale's body.

2. Add in the fins and tail. Sketch in the head and curve of the body.

3. Position the small eye just behind and below the wide mouth. Join the body to the tail. Smooth out the line of the dorsal fin on the whale's back.

4. Give the side fin a bumpy edge. Draw small knobs, called tubercles, around the mouth. Shape the tail and front fin.

5. Paint your whale in a dark blue with a white and pale blue belly. Add some speckles on the side, fins, and head.

TOP TIP

Bring out the tiny bumps on the humpback's head by giving them their own shadows and highlights. The bumps above the mouth follow three curved lines.

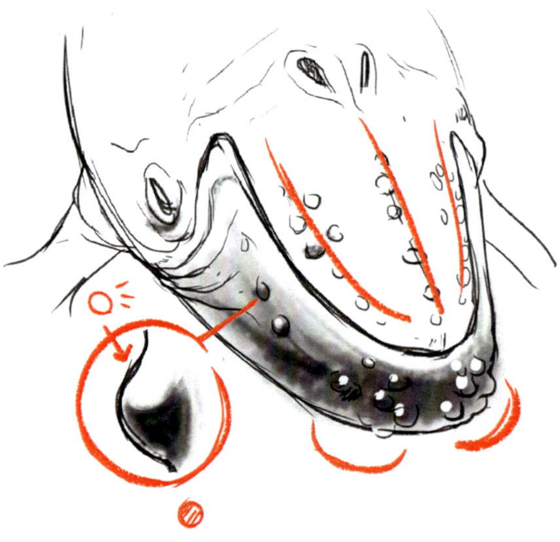

NARWHAL

This unusual whale has a long, spike-shaped tusk on the front of its head.

1. Draw an oval at an angle, with a curved tail on the left.

2. Add a long spike on the right. Draw lines for side fins and mark the head. Add the tail fin.

3. Shape the pair of rounded side fins, then position the small eye just behind the narwhal's wide mouth.

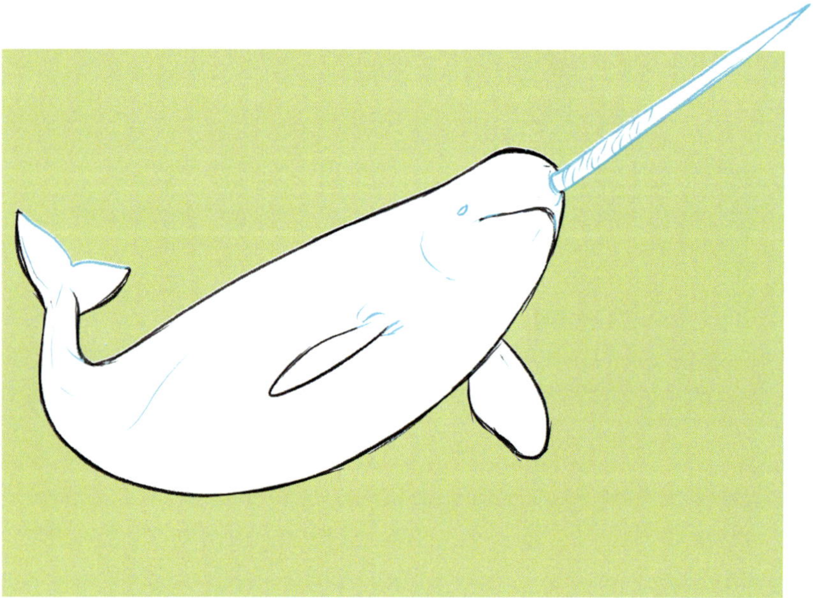

4. Shape the narwhal's tail, then add thickness to the tusk. Draw short lines up the length of the tusk for a spiral effect.

5. Lightly mark the areas of dark and light on the narwhal. It has dark side fins and a very spotty pattern over its body.

TOP TIP

When creating the speckled pattern on the narwhal, go from large spots to smaller ones as you cross into the half with a different shade. Then, repeat in the opposite direction with the other shade.

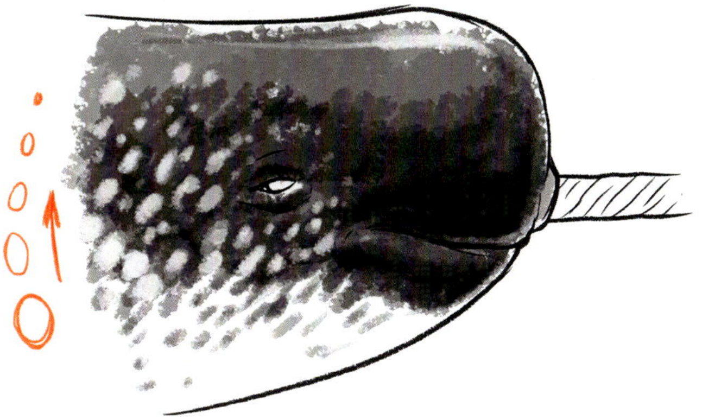

6. Use dark blue paint on the upper half of the narwhal and pale blue on the belly. Use these same shades to add spots on the opposite halves.

GREAT WHITE SHARK

One of the ocean's most powerful predators has a fearsome presence.

1. Draw a basic fish shape with a wide midsection. Indicate the tail fin.

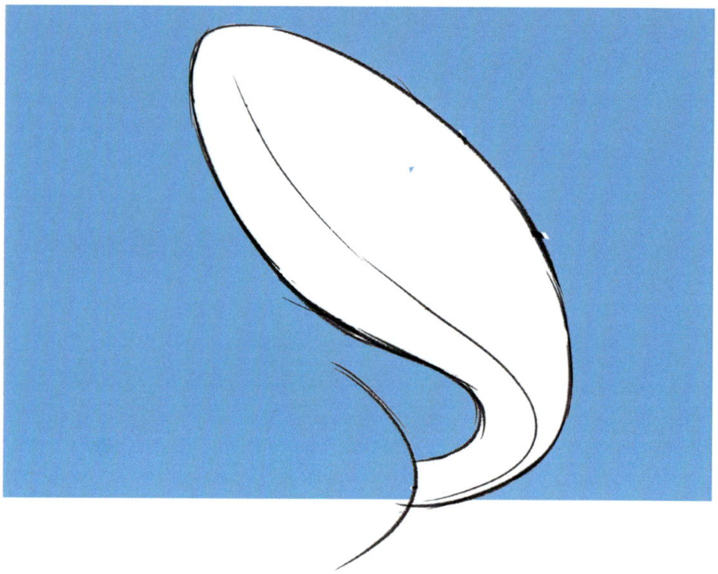

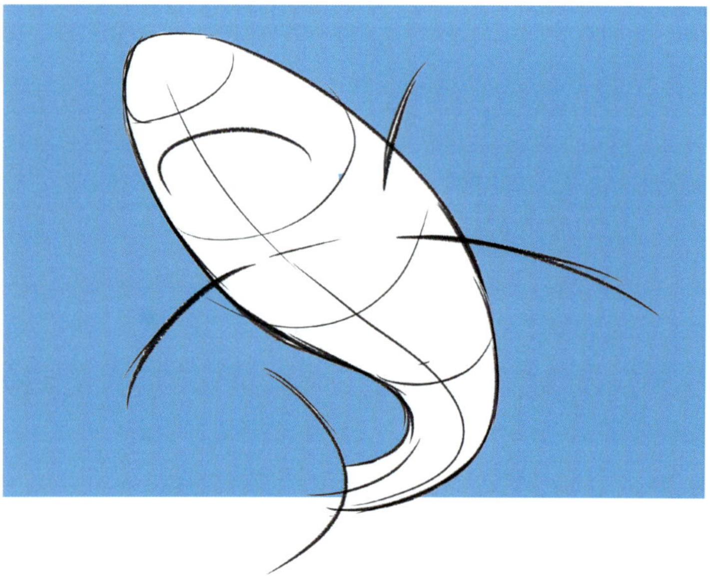

2. Mark where the back and side fins join the body, and also mark a mouth.

3. Shape the triangular fins and tail. Draw the outline of the open mouth, and place the eye.

4. Add the teeth, a pair of large nostrils, and the gill slits in front of the side fin. Note the four small fins near the tail.

TOP TIP

The great white shark has rows of jagged teeth that slowly move forward to replace those that break or fall out. You can draw these smaller extra teeth behind the front rows.

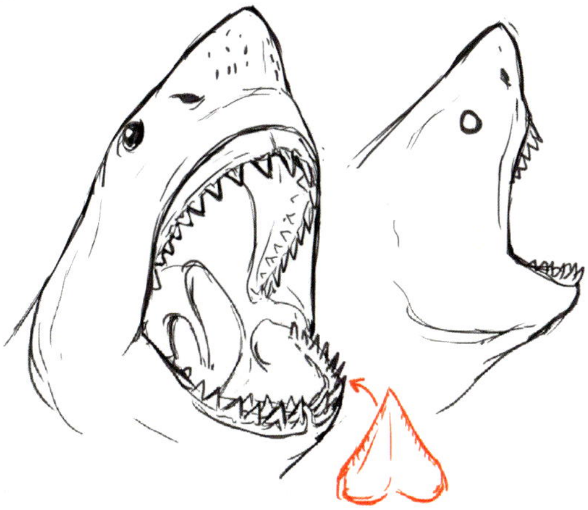

5. Paint your shark with shades of blue, using a paler shade for the belly and dark pink for the gums.

WHALE SHARK

The world's largest fish eats some of the sea's smallest creatures.

1. Start with a basic fish shape with a wide-open mouth.

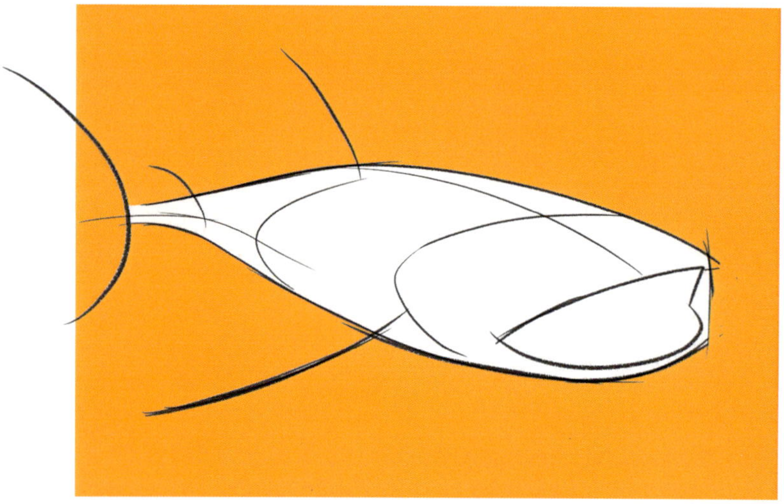

2. Draw lines to indicate the position of the fins and tail.

3. Shape the back and side fins. Sketch a small eye at the side of the whale shark's mouth.

4. Complete the tail, then add three long lines along the body, gill slits behind the eye, and detail inside the mouth.

5. The whale shark has a spotted pattern, with white spots in bands from the tail and random spots on the head and fins.

6. Paint the upper side of the whale shark shades of brown with white spots. The belly is white and has the reflection of the blue sea.

WILD FACT!

The whale shark swims with its mouth open to take in millions of tiny plankton every day. It filters the water to pick out its food.

BASKING SHARK

This giant, harmless shark swims near the surface with a wide, gaping mouth.

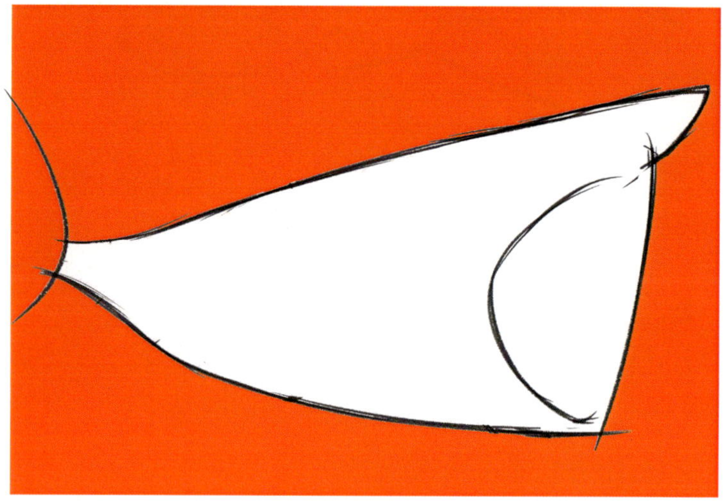

1. Start with a funnel-shaped body, with a wide-open mouth and pointed nose.

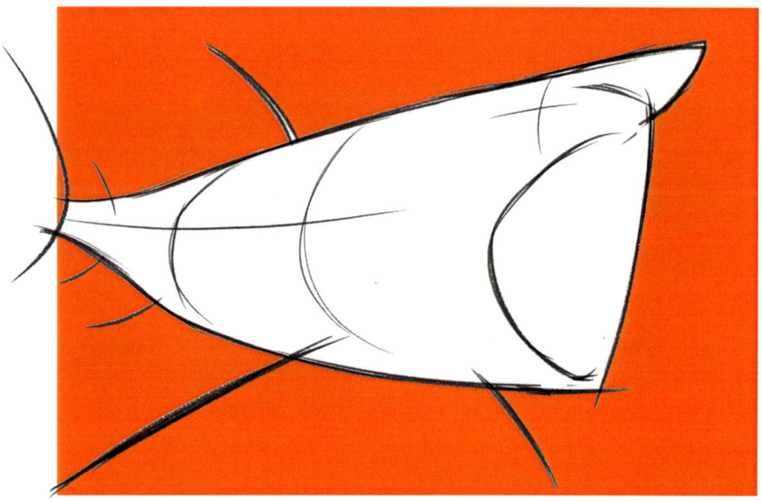

2. Mark the positions of the long pectoral and dorsal fins.

3. Shape the triangular fins and huge mouth. Position the eye above the mouth.

4. Draw curving gill slits halfway along the body, a nostril, and detail inside the mouth.

TOP TIP

You may want to draw the same animal from different angles. It can be helpful to imagine rotating your picture to work out what you would see.

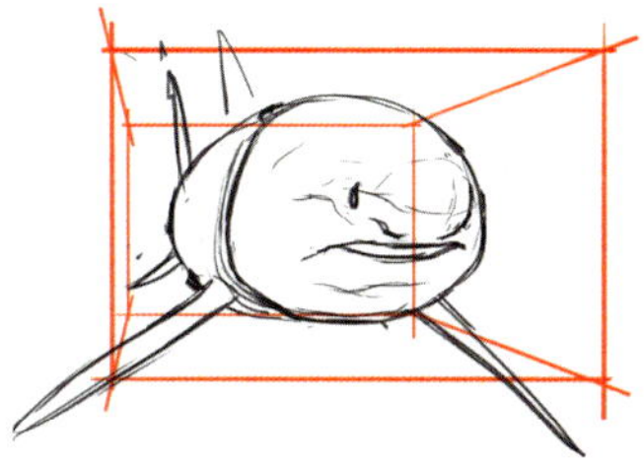

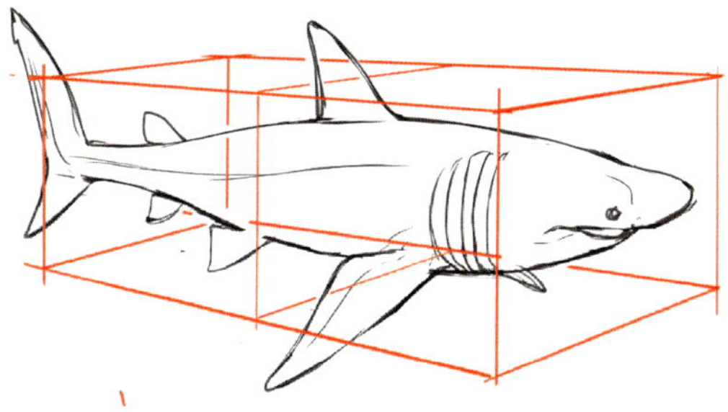

5. Paint your shark, adding a mottled pattern to the sides and back. There are bluish tones inside the large mouth.

GLOSSARY

bizarre Very strange or peculiar.

dorsal fin The fin of a marine animal that sits on its back.

fearsome Frightening or scary.

gill slit One of the many openings of the gills. Animals with gills can breathe underwater.

marine Relating to the sea.

notch An indentation.

pectoral fin The fin of a marine animal that sits on the side of the body.

plankton Microscopic organisms that are often eaten by large marine animals by filtering the water.

predator An animal that hunts other animals for food.

prey An animal that is hunted for food.

symmetrical When two objects look like the mirror image of one another.

tubercle A small round growth that sits on skin or bone.

tusk A long, pointed object.

wrinkle A fold or line in something, such as skin.

FURTHER INFORMATION

Books:

Cuddy, Robbin. *Learn to Draw Sea Creatures.* Lake Forest, CA: Walter Foster Publishing, 2015.

DuBosque, Doug. *Draw Animals: Ocean – Rainforest – Desert – Grassland.* Vancouver, WA: Peel Productions, Inc, 2015.

Gowen, Fiona. *How to Draw Incredible Sharks and Other Ocean Giants.* Hauppauge, NY: Barron's Educational Series, 2016.

McCurry, Kristen. *How to Draw Incredible Ocean Animals.* North Mankato, MN: Capstone Press, 2013.

Websites:

PowerKids Press has developed an online list of websites related to the subject of this book. This site is updated regularly. Please use this link to access the list: www.powerkidslinks.com/aaaa/whalessharksanddolphins

INDEX